Ladybird Readers

The Big Fish

Notes to teachers, parents, and carers

The *Ladybird Readers* Starter Level gently introduces children to the phonics approach to reading, by covering familiar themes that young readers will have studied (for example, colors, animals, and family).

Phonics focuses on how the individual sounds of letters are blended together to sound out a word. For example, /c/ /a/ /t/ when put together sound out the word **cat**.

The Starter Level is divided into two sub-level sections:
- **A** looks at simple words, such as **ant**, **dog**, and **red**.
- **B** explores trickier sound–letter combinations, such as the **/igh/** sound in **night** and **fright**.

This book looks at the theme of **sea animals** and focuses on these sounds and letters: s t ea ai ay

There are some activities to do in this book. They will help children practice these skills:

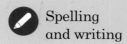 Spelling and writing   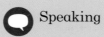 Speaking   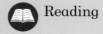 Reading

LADYBIRD BOOKS

UK | USA | Canada | Ireland | Australia
India | New Zealand | South Africa

Ladybird Books is part of the Penguin Random House group of companies
whose addresses can be found at global.penguinrandomhouse.com.
www.penguin.co.uk   www.puffin.co.uk   www.ladybird.co.uk

Penguin
Random House
UK

First published 2017
001

Copyright © Ladybird Books Ltd, 2017

Printed in China
A CIP catalogue record for this book is available from the British Library

ISBN: 978-0-241-29915-9

All correspondence to:
Ladybird Books
Penguin Random House Children's
80 Strand, London WC2R 0RL

The Big Fish

Look at the story

Series Editor: Sorrel Pitts
Story by Coleen Degnan-Veness
Illustrated by Chris Jevons

Picture words

Max

May

boat

sail

fish

tail

long

Aa Bb Cc Dd Ee Ff Gg Hh Ii Jj Kk Ll Mm

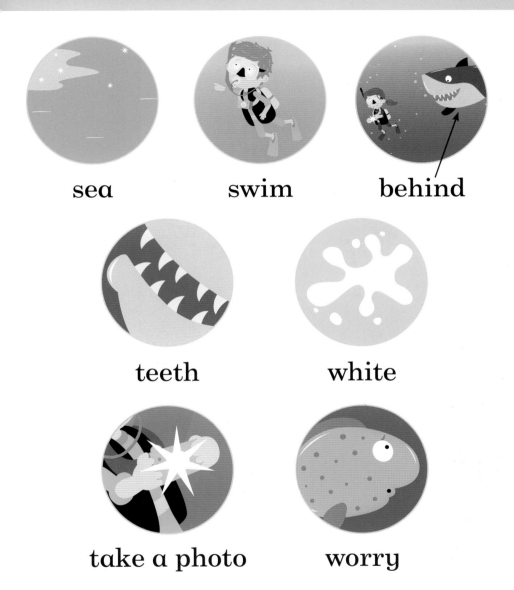

sea

swim

behind

teeth

white

take a photo

worry

Use these words to help you with the activity on page 16.

Nn Oo Pp Qq Rr Ss Tt Uu Vv Ww Xx Yy Zz

Max   May   boat   sail

fish   sea

sea   swim

8

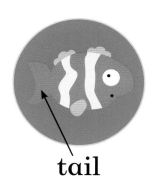

tail

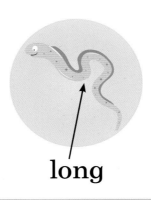

long

take a photo

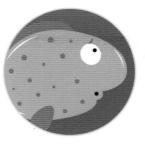

worry

behind

swim   white   teeth

Activity

1   **Color in blue the words with the sound *s*. Color in yellow the words with the sound *t*.**

swim

sail

tail

sea

teeth

The Big Fish

Read the story

Max and May's boat has got two white sails.

19

Max likes the sea.

I can swim with the fish!

May sees a big fish.

A very big fish swims behind May.

May! That big fish wants to eat YOU! Let's go!

25

Max and May swim to the boat.

Activities

2 **Read the sentences.**
Write the letters. 📖 ✏️

ay	ai	ea

1  "Let's find some fish!" s_ay_ Max and May.

2  Their boat has got two white s____ls.

3  "What a nice tail!" says M____.

4  Max likes the s____.

5  "What a very long t____l!" says May.

3 Look and read. Match.

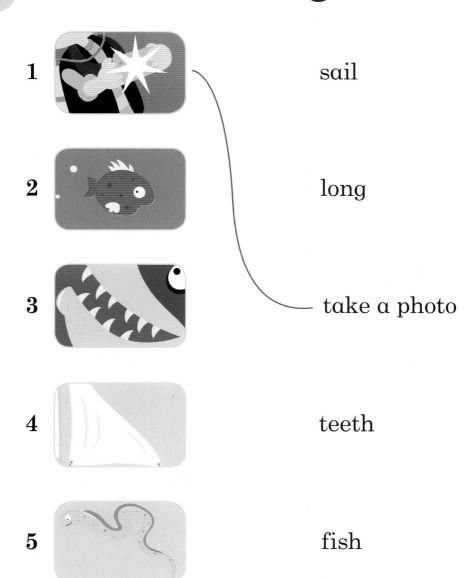

1   sail

2   long

3   take a photo

4   teeth

5   fish

4 Look. Write the letters. Say the words.

1   l   a   i   s

s a i l

2   s   w   m   i

3   a   y   M

4   e   a   s

5   l   a   i   t

30

5 **Look. Say the words.**
Put a ✓ **or a** ✗ **in the boxes.**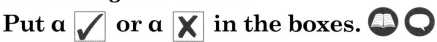

1 boat ✓

2 fish ☐

3 long tail ☐

4 white teeth ☐

5 take a photo ☐

Starter Level A and B

Starter A

The Zoo

978–0–241–28346–2 ☐

Starter A

Dom Dog and his Boat

978–0–241–28340–0 ☐

Starter A

Ted in Bed

978–0–241–28342–4 ☐

Starter A

The Fun Run

978–0–241–28343–1 ☐

Starter A

Nicky and Poppy

978–0–241–29912–8 ☐

Starter B

Doctor Panda

978–0–241–28339–4 ☐

Starter B

Farmer Carl

978–0–241–28341–7 ☐

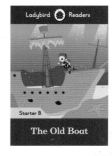

Starter B

The Old Boat

978–0–241–28345–5 ☐

Starter B

Brother Blue

978–0–241–28338–7 ☐

Starter B

In the Mud

978–0–241–29913–5 ☐

Starter B

The Big Fish

978–0–241–29915–9 ☐

Starter B

Gus is Hot!

978–0–241–29914–2 ☐